Julia Jones' Diary

My Worst Day Ever!

Katrina Kahler

Table of Contents

This is how it all started...

The last thing I remember is the look of horror on the faces of the audience. But what had caused me to feel the most humiliation was when I noticed Blake Jansen, the coolest boy in our class, staring down at me in disbelief.

My memory of that night still fills me with shame. Everyone says that I was lucky to get away with only a mild concussion and a huge lump on my head. But the disgrace I had felt at being the laughing stock of the whole school was still very fresh in my mind.

I'd really like to try and forget that entire day, erase it from my memory banks forever, but right now it keeps coming back to haunt me. Loser with a capital L! That's the way I feel about myself right now. I still can't believe the events of that fateful day. If only it were a nightmare I could wake up from and never ever have to think about again. But unfortunately, that is just not the case!

Mom says that time heals all wounds and that everyone else has probably completely forgotten the incident, but I think it's going to take quite a while for me to get over it. For some reason though, I suspect that one particular girl in our class had something to do with it all. Call it gut instinct or intuition, but I have a sneaking suspicion that somehow she was involved.

Thinking back before that doomed day, life had been pretty good. My best friend, Millie and I had auditioned for the school musical and we were both selected for major roles. Being in grade seven gave us an advantage over the younger kids, that and of course the fact that we were both dancers.

The best part was that we'd also been asked to choreograph

sections of the performance and this was a huge honor.

Miss Sheldon, the performing arts teacher who was in charge of the production, had given us the responsibility of coming up with some routines and teaching the other kids the dance moves they needed to learn. We were so excited about this, especially because we'd been left in charge. Miss Sheldon is the coolest teacher ever!

There are some great dancers in our grade; even some of the boys are particularly good. One boy named Alex has been dancing pretty much his entire life and is probably the best dancer in the whole school. When he was younger, he said that the other kids had bullied him and called him a girl as well as a heap of horrible names that he really didn't want to mention. But I could see that everyone had finally developed a huge amount of respect for Alex and those who were still unaware of his talents were in for a big surprise. Hip hop is his specialty and he's so cool to watch. I kept telling him that when he's old enough, he should audition for 'So You Think You Can Dance,' and he told me that he'd really like to.

As well as Alex, there's another kid in our grade who is kind of overweight and dorky looking. But it turns out that he has an awesome voice.

I had no idea that our school has so much talent and it certainly came as a huge surprise to find out that Liam can actually sing really well. The look of amazement when we heard his audition pretty much spread like wild fire. I even caught the teachers raising their eyebrows in astonishment.

It just goes to show you that you can't judge a book by its cover! I never really understood what that meant until hearing Liam sing. Now, I don't think I'll ever look at him in the same way again. It's also a really big lesson for me. From now on, I will never judge a person by their looks alone. I'll wait till I get to know them because I've found out that until you do get to know people, you really don't know what type of person they are or what hidden talents they might have.

Anyway, the musical was shaping up to be a huge success. The dance troupe we had put together was really coming along and we rehearsed during every lunch break and sometimes even after school. Then one afternoon, an amazing thing happened; Blake Jansen, who I've had a secret crush on since the fourth grade, turned up at rehearsals with his friend, Jack.

At first I was embarrassed to see them watching us and to make matters worse, some of the girls actually starting to giggle and carry on. One girl was even fluttering her eyelashes! I'd heard about that sort of thing but had never seen it in action before. Talk about humiliating! I just tried to ignore the boys at first but after about ten minutes of observing our routine, they walked towards Millie and I and actually asked if they could join in.

I couldn't believe it! Blake Jansen really wanted to join our dance troupe! I was sure it was because Alex was involved and everyone was starting to hear how cool he was. But I didn't care about the reason. Having a couple more boys included would just make it so much better! Although, I was reluctant to admit to myself that I was particularly glad one of the boys just happened to be Blake.

Blake

Millie grinned at me and whispered quietly, "Julia...can you believe Blake is joining us!" I pretended I didn't hear her and went into a spiel telling the boys that if they wanted to be involved, they'd have to commit to rehearsals and put in one hundred per cent effort.

Much to my surprise, they were really enthusiastic about the whole thing and couldn't wait to get started. I thought it was awesome they were keen to take part. And surprisingly enough, they turned out to be pretty good. It was shaping up to be a highlight of the musical and I began to really look forward to every rehearsal. Of course having Blake there helped to keep my enthusiasm levels high but I just had to make sure I didn't give him too much attention. I didn't want him thinking that I actually liked him. That would just be too embarrassing!

But, apart from Blake Jansen and constant rehearsals, I really had no idea what was ahead for us. If I had only known at the time, I probably would never have volunteered to take part in the musical at all.

The new girl...

The weeks passed by and school went on as usual. However, as the final performance day drew closer, our practice sessions became more frequent and we were kept very busy.

Millie and I had been asked to choreograph the dance routines for several additional scenes as well, so we had little time for anything else.

Then one morning, just as the bell was ringing and everyone was heading into class, a very pretty girl with blonde wavy hair who looked to be about our age, happened to arrive at our classroom door.

"Come in, Sara!" I heard Mrs. Jackson call out in a friendly manner. "I've been expecting you!"

Everyone looked curiously in the girl's direction. "Girls and boys, I'd like you to meet Sara Hamilton. She has just enrolled at our school and will now be joining our class."

Sara smiled shyly as she followed Mrs. Jackson towards an empty desk next to mine.

"Julia, I'm sure you'll be happy to look after Sara and show her around the school during break times today. Please make her welcome."

"Yes of course, Mrs. Jackson," I answered with enthusiasm as I smiled encouragingly towards Sara. "Hi, Sara! My name's Julia and this is my friend, Millie," I added, pointing towards Millie who was seated on the other side of me.

Millie smiled brightly and jumped up to help Sara unpack her bag and put her books and other belongings into her desk drawer. It was an unusual event to have a new student come to our school and when it happened it was always very exciting. I could see all the other kids in the class looking towards Sara with interest and by the time the bell rang for morning break, Sara was surrounded by girls who were desperately keen to meet her.

We all headed down the stairs towards the area where the grade seven kids sat to eat their morning tea. There was a large group trying to get Sara's attention, so Millie and I sat back in order to avoid overwhelming the poor girl who was swamped with people asking her questions.

As I looked around, I realized that she also had the attention of pretty much every other kid in the grade, the boys included.

Sara was very pretty and was wearing the coolest clothes. I noticed her white sandals; they had straps around the ankles and chunky heels, the latest in fashion and very expensive.

I also realized that she was wearing the pleated suede skirt I had been eyeing off in the window of a local designer store on the weekend. Judging by the reaction of all the girls, I could tell that she was going to be very popular and I wondered suddenly if she was good at dancing.

When the opportunity arose, Millie and I moved closer to Sara and began chatting. She was super friendly and seemed really nice. We found out that she and her family had just moved into town the week before, as her dad had been transferred to a new job in the area.

Sara told us how much she had been looking forward to starting at a new school. She didn't say too much but I kind of got the feeling that the kids at her last school weren't very nice to her. I reassured her that she wouldn't have that problem at our school as all the girls in our class got on really well.

"I've noticed that there are some cute boys here as well," she said to Millie and I with a huge grin.

We grinned back and Millie said, "Yeah, some of them are ok!" with a wink in my direction. I could see that Sara was watching my reaction to Millie's comment and I couldn't help but blush. Trying to change the subject I asked Sara, "Do you like dancing?"

"Oh, I love dancing!" she exclaimed. "It's my favorite thing to do. I was taking hip hop classes before I left my old school and I'm really keen to start up again."

"Oh wow!" I replied. "If you're good at hip hop, you could probably join in our hip hop dance for the musical. It's in four weeks, so you'd have time to learn the routine. Do you want to come to rehearsals at lunch time?"

"I'd love to!" Sara answered. "Thank you so much for inviting me."

"That's alright," I beamed in response. "I'll just have to check with Miss Sheldon but I'm sure it will be fine. She's keen to have as many kids involved as possible."

Chatting excitedly, we headed back to class, explaining what the musical was about and the different dances that Millie and I had choreographed. "It's going to be the most awesome thing ever!" Millie gasped. "The costumes are amazing and we can hardly wait for the night to come."

"This is really cool!" Sara grinned excitedly. "I had a feeling about this school. I knew that it was going to be the right place for me."

As we walked up the stairs, I felt a shiver of excitement run down my spine. "What an unexpected surprise," I thought to myself. I certainly hadn't expected to be making a cool new friend when I arrived at school that morning.

And with beaming smiles, the three of us headed towards our desks and sat down to get on with the work that Mrs. Jackson had put on the board.

Feeling a bit jealous...

It turned out that Sara was very good at hip hop. Actually, she was not just good, she was pretty incredible. The moves that she knew how to do were some that I had never seen before and she was extremely flexible as well. I looked on in amazement while she demonstrated a routine that she'd been working on before she left her old school.

As I glanced around our group, I noticed that everyone else was also looking on in awe. It was hard not to. Her blonde pigtails swung from side to side as she flipped and turned. And the cargo green outfit that she wore was so cool, a perfect hip hop style that matched her clear complexion and blonde hair beautifully.

I glanced down at my shabby shorts that I had quickly changed into before rehearsal and for the first time felt aware of how uncool they were. Usually I didn't worry too much about things like that, especially just for a rehearsal. But having Sara in our midst, looking so perfect, really made me think twice about the way I was dressed.

When she finished, everyone congratulated her and told her how amazing she was. She certainly deserved it and I thought about how lucky we were to have her join us. By incorporating some of the moves that she knew, our dance was sure to be a stand out performance.

We decided to get Sara to demonstrate and everyone was concentrating quite intensely as some of the interchanges were very tricky. Then just when I thought everyone had got the hang of it, Sara stepped over next to Blake and grabbed his arms to show him how he should be moving them.

"It's more this type of action, Blake!" she explained to him as he looked at her with those big brown eyes of his, following her demonstration closely.

"You've almost got it, you just need to make your movements more abrupt and deliberate," she continued.

And when he suddenly mimicked her movements to perfection her squeal was full of obvious delight. "That's it!" she cried. "That's perfect!"

Sara

And with a proud grin, Blake replied, "Thanks heaps, Sara! Thanks for your help." Then obviously very pleased with himself, he continued with the remainder of the routine before joining in with the rest of us to put the new version of our dance together.

"That's such a cool dance, Sara!" Alex exclaimed when we had finally finished. "It's awesome to have a girl who's so good at hip hop at our school."

"Yeah, that was great, Sara," Jack chimed in, obviously not wanting to miss out on getting her attention.

"Thanks!" Sara replied in a modest manner. "You guys are really good dancers too!"

As I packed up my gear and headed on over towards them, I couldn't help but notice the smile on Blake's face as he chatted easily with Sara. They looked like they were getting on really well. And as I watched her talking happily with the group of boys, I guessed that Sara would probably get along with just about everyone.

Something feels wrong...

"Oh my gosh!" Millie exclaimed. "Look who's sitting down at a table in McDonald's right now!"

I followed the direction of Millie's gaze where to my surprise, I spotted Blake, Jack and Alex, the three boys from our dance troupe at school. Their undivided attention was cast towards a girl whose back was towards us. But I knew that I would recognize that flowing long, blonde hair anywhere.

"What are they all doing here together?" asked Millie, curiously.

"I have no idea!" I replied, "But let's go find out." And I strode quickly over towards their table.

Millie and I had decided to spend Saturday afternoon at the mall. I'd had my eye on a really pretty top that had recently come into stock in my favorite store and I had decided I would use my birthday money to buy it. However, to my huge dismay, on entering the store a few minutes earlier, I had discovered that there were none left in my size.

When Millie realized how hugely disappointed I was, she offered to buy me a thick shake at McDonalds to try and cheer me up. That was when we happened to notice our friends from school.

"Hey guys," I said in a friendly manner. "What are you all doing here?"

They had been so absorbed in Sara's conversation, that they had not seen us approach and got quite a start at the unexpected sound of my voice.

"Julia!" Sara exclaimed, "And Millie! What a surprise to see you here." They all shuffled over to make room at the booth for us and although the boys welcomed us without hesitation, I kind of got the impression that Sara did not feel the same way. An uncomfortable tension seemed to appear out of nowhere but then I decided I must be imagining things. So I started chatting aimlessly about it being such a coincidence to run into each other like that. The boys explained that they had been to see a movie and had then bumped into Sara afterwards, just as they were entering McDonalds.

"I was shopping with my mom," Sara said. "When I saw the boys, Mom told me I could meet up with her in about half an hour so I could have some time to hang out with them."

Grinning in Blake's direction she continued, "The boys said they might even come to my house tomorrow so we can do some extra rehearsals. You girls can come as well if you want, but if you're too busy, then that's ok. We can just practice at school on Monday."

"I can't make it tomorrow," replied Millie, obviously disappointed. "We're going to visit my grandparents so I'll be out for the whole day."

"Oh, that's too bad!" answered Sara. "Never mind, we can all get together on Monday."

"Julia can probably go, though," Millie quickly responded. "You were saying earlier that you had nothing to do tomorrow, Julia!"

Looking towards Sara, I replied, "Only if that's ok with you, Sara."

"Oh, that's fine, Julia. Of course you can come. I'm planning on teaching the boys some other dance moves that I know.

17

So I can teach you too, if you like."

"That sounds great," I answered, trying to muster some enthusiasm. For some reason though, I didn't feel completely welcome and sat there quietly while Sara continued her animated conversation; with the boys as her main audience.

I suddenly noticed a familiar looking carry bag sitting on the seat between myself and Sara and then recognized it as coming from my favorite clothing store.

"Have you been shopping at Dream Warehouse?" I asked Sara curiously. "That's my favorite store."

"Yes," Sara replied brightly. "I just bought the prettiest top, only about fifteen minutes ago. As soon as I saw it, I just had to have it and I'm so lucky because it was the last one in my size! Do you like it?" she asked, pulling it out of the bag.

I gasped in surprise when I realized that it was the exact same top that I had intended to buy for myself and when I looked at it more closely, I spotted the label and realized that it was also in my size. Sara had beaten me to it. "What are the chances of that?" I sighed to myself as I commented on how pretty it was.

I decided not to mention that I had actually planned on buying that very top, but then out of the blue, Millie exclaimed, "Sara, that looks like the top you wanted to buy. Isn't it exactly the same one? And it's in your size as well!"

Seeing my expression, Sara responded, "Oh Julia, did I beat you to it? I'm so sorry!"

For some reason, I felt that she really wasn't being sincere, but I told her not to worry about it and decided to put it out of my mind. I didn't know what was bugging me. "Perhaps

I'm coming down with something?" I wondered. "Or maybe I'm just being silly. Sara is a really nice girl, it's obvious how much everyone likes her and we're really lucky to have her in our class."

As Millie and I sat on the bus heading home later that afternoon, I decided to push all the crazy thoughts about Sara from my mind. We really were fortunate to have her come to our school and to actually have her talent included in our dance troupe was something to be very grateful for.

I decided to focus on attempting some new hip hop moves myself that I could share with the guys the next day and tried to remove all the uneasy thoughts from my mind. But for some reason, I just couldn't shake the foreboding premonition that seemed to be tingling down my spine.

Envy...

As I lay in bed on Sunday night, thinking about the afternoon that I had spent at Sara's house, the previous thoughts that I'd been having on my way home from the mall the day before, were furthest from my mind.

It turned out that the boys couldn't make it as some other stuff had apparently come up, but in the end I was glad. It was so nice to spend time alone with Sara and I found that when it was just the two of us, we got along really well.

She lives in the coolest house. It's really big and super modern. They even have a spa bath in the bathroom as well as a jacuzzi out by the pool. We talked about spending time sunbathing in her backyard as soon as the weather was warm enough. The lounge chairs that were scattered around the sides of the pool were so inviting that I had to try them out. Then when I found that they reclined right back, I laid there picturing myself during the summer months, just relaxing by that beautiful sparkling pool.

Sara is so lucky! She seems to have pretty much everything a girl could wish for. Her bedroom has the prettiest pink wallpaper with a gorgeous white flower print as a feature wall. And her furniture is all white. She has a huge comfy bed with matching bedside tables. I've never known a girl our age to have a queen sized bed though. Even my parents only have a double bed and Sara's bed seems enormous in comparison.

The two hot pink chrome lamps that sit on her bedside tables are the coolest design and I just love the fluffy pink rug that spreads across the middle of her floor. And she even has a window seat that looks out through a big white framed window, across the landscaped back yard and pool area. I've always dreamed of having a window seat like that, it's just like in the movies.

It's pretty difficult not to feel just a little bit jealous of Sara though. She has so much cool stuff and she is so pretty. But I guess being an only child is the reason why her parents spoil her so much. It would probably be hard not to spoil an only child. I only met her mom briefly but she seems very nice. Although, Sara said that her parents are rarely at home and I was actually lucky to meet her mother. Apparently her dad's office is in town but he has to travel a lot and her mom is always out doing something or other, Sara isn't really sure what.

I thought that was pretty strange; not really knowing what your mom does every day and hardly seeing your parents. Sara said that it's good not having parents to annoy her because she can do whatever she wants when they're not around. It's a bit of a weird situation, but I guess everyone is different.

They're certainly very different to my family, that's for sure. There's no way I'd be allowed to have all that freedom! My parents want to know what I'm up to all the time. They check on where I am and what time I will be home and who I am spending time with. And we always eat meals together, breakfast and dinner anyway; as well as that, we have regular family time where we play board games or watch a movie or go on an outing together somewhere.

My brother, Matt is getting sick of family time and often complains because he would rather be hanging out with his friends. I guess boys his age are like that, but I still like being around my family.

I rolled over and stared out the window and into the night sky. There was a full moon shining and its light was beaming into my room, making it hard for me to go to sleep. I didn't want to close the curtain though, as I love watching the stars at night time, especially from the comfort of my bed.

As I finally started to drift off, visions of Sara came to mind. She was dressed in the most incredible hip hop outfit and was bowing to applause from an adoring audience, her wide smile beaming across her face. I pictured myself sitting amongst the crowd and cheering her on as well.

Then abruptly, I sat up with a start. A cold shiver had run right through me and I could feel the hairs on my arms standing on end. Unsure of what had caused the sudden disturbing feeling, I looked around my room and realized the window was wide open so I jumped up to close it. Hopping back into bed, I rolled over and closed my eyes. We had an early rehearsal planned in the morning before school so I needed to get up early. I pulled the covers up to my chin and fell into a deep sleep.

The take-over begins...

Our early morning rehearsal didn't turn out quite as I had expected.

When I arrived at the prearranged time, I was very surprised to see Sara and the rest of the gang already there and by the look of their sweat drenched faces, it appeared that they'd been practicing for quite some time already.

"Where have you been?" Alex asked. "Did you miss the bus or something?"

Looking confused, I checked the time on my watch. "I thought we'd arranged to start at eight am," I replied. "And that's still five minutes away."

"Hey guys!" called Millie as she approached from behind me. "Have you already started?"

I looked from Millie to Alex to Sara and then to the rest of the group, shaking my head in confusion. I could see that Blake had a weird look on his face but then Sara's voice broke the silence.

"Oh, Julia!" she exclaimed. "I called Blake last night and we decided to get an early start. I thought that someone would have contacted you girls to let you know."

Blake frowned and looked in Sara's direction, obviously confused about what she was saying. But without missing a beat, she continued, "Well, never mind! You're here now, so why don't you just join in? We've made a few changes to the routine. I hope you like it. Everyone else thinks it's really cool!"

Glancing towards Millie who was shrugging her shoulders

as if to indicate that she had no idea what was going on, we stood back and watched as everyone demonstrated what they'd been working on.

"The guys are keen for me to be in the lead at the front," Sara explained, while trying to catch her breath after they'd finished what I had to admit was a very impressive routine.

I looked around at the group and they all seemed to be looking in any direction except towards me. So I replied in a quiet voice, "Well, if that's what everyone wants, then I guess that's how we'll do the dance."

Trying to muster some enthusiasm, I joined Millie in the second row to rehearse the new moves a few more times. All the while, my head was spinning.

"I know I'm not in charge," I thought frantically to myself, "And everyone should certainly have a say in what we do. But I'm really not sure what's going on here!"

"Ok!" called Sara brightly, about ten minutes later as she suddenly called the rehearsal to a close. "That was great guys. This new routine is really coming together. Let's meet up again early tomorrow morning. Julia and Millie, do you think you can make it? If we all arrive by seven-thirty, we'll have plenty of time for a good rehearsal!"

And without even waiting for an answer, she strode off towards the locker room, to have a quick shower before heading to class.

"What just happened?" Millie whispered, a frown of misunderstanding still very evident on her face.

"I have no idea!" I replied and then followed her into the locker room so we could also get showered and changed before the bell went.

Walking slowly back to class, I watched Sara striding alongside Blake, just ahead of Millie and I, chatting away in her usual animated manner. Then when we sat down at our desks, she smiled towards me as if nothing unusual whatsoever had happened. I looked at Mrs. Jackson who had begun explaining a new Math concept but found it very difficult to concentrate. Visions of the morning's rehearsal were floating around in my head and I could not get Sara's confident voice out of my mind.

"Julia!" Mrs. Jackson repeated for the second time. "Are you listening or not?"

"I have just said your name three times and you still aren't answering my question. Would you rather do this work during break time?"

"Sorry, Mrs. Jackson!" I replied in a worried tone, "Is the answer twenty-two?"

"Oh my goodness, Julia!" she explained. "You haven't been listening to a word I've said. I think you'd better stay behind and complete this activity during morning tea break. Maybe then you'll decide to concentrate!"

Glancing towards Millie, I felt grateful for her genuine look of sympathy but the grin that remained on Sara's face was not something I had expected to see and a worried knot started to form in the pit of my stomach.

Am I being paranoid?...

Sitting at the dinner table that night, I didn't feel very hungry at all. I sat there picking at my food, while my brother, Matt went on and on about the goal he had scored at footy training that afternoon.

As if I was interested in his football game! I really don't like football at all and was so glad that I didn't have to suffer being dragged along to his training sessions and games anymore. Finally, I'm old enough to stay at home on my own, rather than facing boredom at the football field every weekend.

My parents however, both love football, especially my dad and they took great interest in Matt's conversation about the season and how well his team were doing in the competition. In a way though, I was glad they had something to occupy them which took their attention away from me as I really didn't feel like talking about the day I'd had.

Morning tea break had consisted of me having to sit at my desk eating the food from my lunchbox, while doing extra Math. That was my punishment for not listening during the morning's lesson.

Then when I was finally allowed to go out, Millie and I had to attend a meeting for the committee in charge of the musical. We were asked to report on the progress of the dances we'd been choreographing and practicing. Then we were informed of a dress rehearsal which was scheduled to take place in two weeks' time and were given information to distribute to everyone.

So overall, it hadn't been the best of days. Although Sara had maintained her friendly manner and continued as if everything were normal, I wasn't so sure. Well, in the scheme of things, I guess everything was ok and I wondered if it were all in my imagination. Was I just being jealous and immature? And was I being a total control freak? Even though I had organized the dances and the choreography, along with Millie's help, it didn't mean that I had to be in charge of our group's dance.

Sara is an exceptional dancer, and I really have to admit that she is very talented. I should be grateful for her support and the way in which our routine has improved since she joined us. But I just couldn't shake the uneasy feeling that I had been overcome with since arriving at rehearsal that morning.

With a dejected sigh, I excused myself from the table under the pretext that I had homework to complete. Luckily my mom was still so absorbed in Matt's excited ramblings that she neglected to remind me it was my turn to do the dishes.

I headed up to my room and tried to concentrate on the homework that was due the following day. More Math! That was certainly not what I felt like doing, but rather than having to face the wrath of my teacher the following morning, I forced myself to concentrate so I could just get it over with.

When I turned out the light a couple of hours later and hopped into bed, I decided that the next day I would join in with everyone else and focus on a good rehearsal. "I'm not going to let Sara bother me," I thought to myself as I closed my eyes. "I'll just be my usual friendly self and I'm sure that everything will be fine!"

We had the school musical to look forward to and it was the highlight of the year so far. I was determined that nothing was going to spoil it!

She's like a Super Hero...

An unexpected surprise awaited us when we entered the school grounds the next morning. Millie and I had caught the same bus and as we were determined to be on time for rehearsal, we raced off the bus and through the school gates in an excited rush.

In the school car park however, where there would normally only be a few cars belonging to teachers at that time of the morning, we discovered several vans parked haphazardly and a large crowd of students milling around trying to find out what was going on.

Pushing through the crowd, curious to find out what had grasped everyone's attention, we spotted two policemen questioning our school principal, Mr. Davis.

Then immediately behind him were a couple of men with large microphones and some sophisticated looking camera equipment. They appeared to be from the local TV station and were interviewing a group of kids. When I managed to get closer, I realized that right in the middle of the group with the microphone pointed directly towards her, was Sara Hamilton.

"It was so scary!" Sara was saying. "But as soon as I heard the smash, I ran to the office to get help."

"You are a very quick thinking young lady!" the reporter acknowledged Sara with a look of admiration.

"Well, I just did what I thought I should," Sara explained. "When I saw the smoke coming from the broken window, I knew that something was terribly wrong!"

"If Sara hadn't acted as quickly as she had, the whole

building could have burnt down!" exclaimed Miss Fitz, the drama teacher who was standing beside her.

"You're very lucky to have such a responsible young lady attending your school!" the reporter who was conducting the interview commented enthusiastically.

Sara, how does it feel to be a hero?

"Yes, we are very proud of Sara, she is new to our school and as you say, we are very lucky to have her here as a student!" chimed in Mr. Davis, beaming with pride in Sara's direction.

The reporters asked Mr. Davis a few more questions and ended the interview. Sara was then quickly surrounded by a surge of kids trying to get close to her in order to be captured on camera. By that time, more kids had arrived for school and the car park was ablaze with excitement. It was not every day that a television camera crew along with several members of the police force turned up, and everyone was keen to get in on the action.

Mr. Dawson, the physical education teacher blew his whistle and told everyone to go to class or wherever they should be at that time of the morning. Then it wasn't until we reached our classroom that Millie and I could actually find out the exact details of what had happened.

Mrs. Jackson explained to us all that Sara had been at school early, in preparation for our dance rehearsal. Apparently as she had walked across the car park, towards the Performing Arts hall, she'd heard a loud smash of glass. When she went around to the rear of the building to investigate, she noticed smoke and flames billowing from the window.

She had then rushed for help and very luckily, had bumped into the janitor who happened to be cleaning the area around the office, which was still fairly deserted at that time of the morning. He and Sara raced back to the building where they'd spotted a couple of teenage boys running from the scene. Between the two of them, Sara and the janitor had managed to get a nearby garden hose connected so they could put out the fire.

Without their quick thinking, the building could have burnt down and that would have been the end of the musical, as it was the only building that was suitable for the performance.

Just as Mrs. Jackson finished sharing the main details, Sara walked into the classroom. Everyone stared in her direction and then a loud burst of applause and cheering erupted. "Three cheers for Sara!" someone at the back of the room called out.

"Hip, Hip, Hooray! Hip, Hip, Hooray! Hip, Hip, Hooray!" the applause was deafening and Sara sat down at her desk, beaming proudly while kids rushed to pat her on the back and give her high fives.

I spotted Blake looking at her with open admiration. She really was a hero and deserved all the accolades she was getting. It would have been disastrous if the building had burnt down. It could even have led to the whole school going up in flames.

As everyone returned to their desks, I congratulated her warmly. She was the most popular girl in the school at that moment and I could see that everyone wanted to be her friend.

When Mrs. Jackson directed us to take out our Math books so we could begin work, I caught Sara smiling happily in Blake's direction. He was grinning widely across the room towards her as well and it was obvious that they had certainly become close. I looked at Millie who had also noticed the exchange and she raised her eyebrows questioningly.

Sara glanced at me with a smug kind of grin, maintaining intense eye contact for a few seconds and then quickly refocused her attention on her math book.

"Pay attention please, Julia! It's time to get on with our lessons now." I heeded Mrs. Jackson's warning and looked towards the board.

It was full of Math equations but once again, I struggled to concentrate. I really wasn't sure whether I had a real friend in Sara or not and began to suspect that she may not be the girl she had so far portrayed herself to be. I then wondered what agenda she had in mind.

As I sat there, I considered the questions racing through my mind. Did I just have an over active imagination or were my instincts picking up on something that was not as it seemed? I guessed that only time would tell!

The birthday party...

Finally it was the weekend. I jumped out of bed early on Saturday morning eager to have breakfast and be ready when Millie arrived to pick me up.

Our week had been very hectic! Since the incident in the Performing Arts building, we were forced to do our rehearsals in a small adjoining room while the damage to the main area was being repaired. And unfortunately, it wasn't free very often so we had to make the most of the limited amount of time that we were given to use it.

Sara's hero status had escalated and as I had predicted, everyone wanted to be her friend. Although I sat next to her in class and she was always polite and reasonably friendly, it seemed that she didn't have time for Millie and I during breaks anymore. She was too preoccupied with all the new friends she had made, including of course, Blake Jansen.

Meanwhile, Millie and I continued to work with the other dance groups and the younger kids whose dances we had to coordinate and choreograph, which kept us pretty busy ourselves.

But now that Saturday had finally arrived, I looked forward with enthusiasm to the day ahead. After a couple of days of heavy rain, the sun was shining and it promised to be a beautiful day. Jackie, one of the girls in our class had invited a group of friends to her house to celebrate her birthday. She lived on a large property that was situated on the outskirts of town. Most of us lived in the suburbs and never got the chance to do all the fun things that are possible when you own lots of land, so we were all really excited about it.

I had been there once for her birthday party years before and

I remembered vividly, the amazing day I had experienced. One of the highlights had been a trailer ride that her dad had taken us all on. He had hooked up their open box trailer to the back of his four wheel drive and everyone had climbed into the back. Even two of our teachers had hopped in with us.

I remembered thinking how lucky Jackie was to have our teachers at her birthday party but now that idea seems pretty ridiculous. Having our current teacher, Mrs. Jackson at a birthday party is not something I could imagine anyone in my class wanting to arrange. It would be different if she were young and cool like Miss Fitz, our drama teacher, but Mrs. Jackson is pretty old now and I don't think that she'd enjoy it either!

There were about twenty kids at the time as well as the teachers, all squashed into the back of that trailer. Although I guess because the kids were quite small, we managed to fit in reasonably well. Everyone had been screaming and cheering as Jackie's dad drove around and around this huge grassy area and up their dirt driveway then back down again. The excitement we felt when he went over bumps on the road or the grass was so intense that none of us had wanted him to stop.

That trailer ride really was a highlight of my childhood and back then, I thought that Jackie was the luckiest kid alive to grow up on a property like that. And reminiscing about that day made me wonder if they still had that trailer because I thought it would still be a pretty cool thing to do!

When I jumped into the back of Millie's car later that morning, I was filled with excited anticipation about what lay ahead. Blake, Jack and Alex had also been invited and it was pretty much all that everyone had been able to talk about at school the day before. Sitting alongside Millie, we chatted about how much fun the party was going to be as well as how we were looking forward to giving Jackie her birthday present. We had gone shopping at the mall after school one day earlier in the week and were so happy with what we had bought.

The light blue jacket studded with silver sequins and a cool design on the collar and cuffs of the sleeves had definitely stood out on the rack. And because we'd had enough money left over from what we had pooled together, we were also able to buy her a really pretty silver necklace with a capital J on it. She had always admired the one I wore, which my mom had given me for my last birthday. It was just very lucky that we had gone shopping when the sales were on as the prices for everything were drastically reduced. That meant we were able to get her an extra special present and we couldn't wait to give it to her!

I
♥
Shopping!

When we jumped out of the car, we saw Jackie running towards us, a huge grin on her face. We were the first to arrive and she was bubbling over with excitement.

We gave her a hug and handed her the present that we had carefully wrapped in shimmering pink paper, along with a darker shade of curling ribbon tied decoratively around it.

She could see our impatience in wanting her to open it straight away but decided to place it on a table on the veranda of her house so that all the presents could be opened later on, when everyone was there together.

While we were waiting for the others, she showed us around her property. Since my last visit, her parents had made some incredible changes to the outside entertaining area of their home. Where there was once just a large patch of green grass, now sat a huge sparkling swimming pool to which was attached an amazing looking diving deck at one end. Although summer had not yet arrived, the temperature that day was unusually warm. In addition, her parents had activated the pool's heating system in preparation for the party so the water would also be a lovely temperature.

There were streamers and balloons strung everywhere including on the walls and framework of a nearby gazebo and this really added to the birthday party atmosphere.

While we waited for the others to arrive, Jackie offered to take us over to the horse paddocks. As well as all the other advantages of living on a property, Jackie also had a pony of her own. He was a beautiful chestnut welsh mountain pony called Charlie and was the cutest thing I had ever seen.

Ever since I was a little girl, I had always dreamed of owning my own pony one day and I gently stroked his forehead, wistfully thinking about how much I would love to have my own horse. He eagerly took the carrots from our hands that Jackie had given us to feed to him and his rough tongue tickled my skin as he licked up the last remnants of carrot that remained.

"You will have to come over more often," Jackie said to us, especially when she realized how taken with her pony we were.

"We'd love to!" Millie and I replied in unison.

"You have the coolest property, Jackie," I continued. "You're so lucky!!"

Jackie smiled in response and then said, "Come on, we'd better head back. The others may be here already!"

We raced towards the house just as several cars were pulling up in the driveway. It seemed that everyone was arriving at once. People were jumping out of cars and within minutes, Jackie was laden with gifts from all her guests. Then I noticed Sara strolling down the driveway with her mom. She had so many items that she needed help to carry it all. And in her hands was a huge box that was gift wrapped in the most beautiful lilac colored wrapping paper with an enormous white bow adorning the top.

"Oh my gosh, Sara!" Jackie exclaimed. "What is inside that parcel?"

"Oh, it's just something small!" Sara replied sweetly. "But I hope you like it!"

Right behind Sara, I saw Blake and his friend, Jack. When Sara spotted them both, I could see her sudden spark of interest.

"Hi boys!" she called out in her usual friendly manner. "Can you please help me with all of this?" And she indicated the gear that her mom was carrying for her. They quickly moved to relieve her of all the bags and bits and pieces and then followed Sara into the house.

Trailing Jackie into her bedroom, the girls all stored their belongings and quickly got changed to go swimming. Because the boys were already dressed in swimming trunks, they had raced straight down to the pool, keen to get into the water. In typical boy style, by the time the girls joined them the boys were already doing bomb dives off the trampoline that stood by the pool's edge.

Squealing with excitement at being splashed, the girls stood by laughing and giggling as they watched the boys in action.

"I'm going to try that too!" Sara exclaimed as she followed

Blake up onto the trampoline.

"Only two are allowed on the trampoline at once," Jackie warned as Alex and a couple of the girls tried to climb up and join in the fun.

"But we can all jump off the diving deck together!" Jackie continued, running around to the other side of the pool and onto the large diving platform.

"This is an awesome setup, Jackie!" called out Sara as she gave Blake a shove into the pool and then bomb dived into the water right next to him.

I stood alongside Millie, watching everyone and in particular, Sara who was paying so much attention to Blake.

It was clearly obvious that she really liked him and it seemed that she wanted him and everyone else to know it.

Grabbing his head, she tried to dunk him under the water but he quickly swam away, jumped out of the pool and back onto the trampoline.

"Show us your biggest bomb dive, Blake," Sara called out, but he just grinned and kept bouncing on the tramp.

"Let's go in," Millie called, grabbing my hand and leading me onto the diving deck.

Holding hands, we ran and did a big jump into the pool together. I was determined to just enjoy myself and not worry about Sara or Blake.

It was shaping up to be a great party and there was too much fun to be had, to be bothered worrying about them.

Just then I noticed Becky, one of the girls from our dance group, sitting on a chair in the gazebo watching everyone in the water.

"Becky!" I called. "Aren't you coming in?" Becky hadn't changed into her swimmers and I wondered why.

Hopping out of the pool, I grabbed my towel and went over to join her. When I asked again why she wasn't swimming, she simply replied that she didn't want to.

By that time, Millie had joined us and quietly whispered in my ear. "She's too embarrassed to put swimmers on."

I looked at Becky with sympathy. She was such a nice girl but had developed a real paranoia about her weight. Even though she wasn't what you would call fat, she had become very self-conscious about her body and I remembered that towards the end of the previous summer she had started declining all offers to go swimming. No one else had commented, but Millie and I had figured out the reason why.

"It's so much fun, Becky and the water is really warm!" I coaxed. "Why don't you put your swimmers on and hop in with us?"

"I forgot to bring them," she explained in a quiet voice.

I knew that she would intentionally have left them behind, but then I suggested that she could borrow a pair from Jackie.

"Oh no, that's ok," she replied. "They probably wouldn't fit me anyway! I'm happy just watching everybody!"

However, I could see that this clearly was not the case. Becky was looking longingly towards the pool, as she sat following the actions of everyone jumping into the water. And when I looked up, I saw them all standing in a row on the diving deck, holding hands ready to take a running jump into the deep end. Sara had a firm hold of Blake's hand on one side and Jack's hand on the other and was calling out, "One, two, three…" after which they all took a flying leap. It looked like so much fun and I was keen to join them myself.

Just then, an idea popped into my head. I whispered quietly in Millie's ear and then indicated for her to follow my lead.

Leaping to my feet, I raced to the side of the pool and called out, "Girls, have a look at this!"

Millie ran over to see what had got my attention and as expected, Becky joined her. When both girls were looking curiously into the water, wondering what I had become so excited about, I sneaked behind the two of them and pushed them both in. Becky was still fully clothed, but I was determined that she should join in the fun. The squeal of surprise that came from her just before she hit the water made everyone look in her direction.

Panicking momentarily at what her reaction would be, I let out a huge sigh of relief when she came to the surface with a grin and exclaimed, "Julia Jones! I'm going to have to get you back for that!"

"Oh well," I replied. "You're all wet now, so you may as well stay in the water!" And I dived in beside her.

Being dressed in shorts and a little singlet top, I knew Becky would be fine to swim as she was. And because we had all brought a change of clothes, I figured she'd have something dry to put on afterwards.

It turned out to be the best thing I could have done as from that moment on, the beaming smile never left her face. And it took very little effort to encourage her to join us in lining up on the diving deck ready for a big jump. She was obviously feeling comfortable as she was fully clothed rather than having to expose her body in a pair of swimmers. But I was glad to see her joining in with the rest of us.

Jackie's mom was there with her camera, ready to take photos and just as we were about to run and leap, I felt someone come around behind me and grab my hand. Looking up in surprise, I saw that it was Blake and laughing, we all held hands and took a running jump.

When we resurfaced, I noticed Sara watching as Blake tried to dunk my head under the water. She was clearly not impressed that he was showing me so much attention and then out of the blue, she suddenly starting screaming, "Oh my head! My head!" All eyes were then abruptly focused on her.

"What's wrong?" Jackie called out in a worried tone. "Are you alright Sara?"

"No!" she replied angrily. "Someone kicked me in the head when I went under water just then! Ouch, it really hurts!"

And she stormed out of the pool and slumped down in a chair in the gazebo.

Everyone else immediately climbed out and went to surround her. Jackie's mom raced inside to get some ice and some of the girls wrapped a towel around her shoulders while trying to comfort her. Millie looked at me and rolled her eyes. "What a drama queen!" she said, shaking her head as she got out of the water and headed towards the trampoline.

I looked back at Sara with puzzlement then decided she had enough people attending to her so I joined Millie on the tramp. We soon became so absorbed in the fun we were having that we didn't realize everyone was leaving the pool area to go inside.

But when a shrill scream abruptly emanated from the direction of the house, we both looked up with a start. "Oh, my gosh!" I exclaimed to Millie. "What was that?"

Anxiously, I jumped off the trampoline and hurriedly followed her towards all the commotion.

The slumber party is hijacked...

The girls were all cowering in a corner of the living room but the reaction from the boys was completely the opposite.

"Oh, wow!" Jack was exclaiming in an excited tone. "This is awesome!"

Hovering as close as they dared to get, they stood transfixed with fascination as they stared agape at the writhing creature that had appeared on the living room floor.

"No, it is not awesome! It is totally freaky!!" Sara's squeal was the loudest of all and was probably the scream that Millie and I had heard when we were out by the pool.

Jackie's parents were nowhere to be seen and then I remembered watching them carry buckets of horse feed over to the back paddock after tending to the bump on Sara's head. So I guessed they were still over there, feeding the horses.

"Have you got a broom?' I asked Jackie as I stood in the doorway, watching the scene in front of me unfold.

It was clear that if something wasn't done quickly, one of the boys was sure to be bitten. The snake that had appeared on the rug in front of us seemed to be getting more agitated by the minute.

Jackie raced to grab a broom which I abruptly grabbed from her hands and held out towards the snake hoping to keep it at bay. We caught a glimpse of the bright red of its underbelly, which contrasted vividly with the shining black scales that covered its back.

Motioning for the girls to move out of the doorway, I tried to coax the snake towards the exit and freedom. Meanwhile, Jackie's cat sat ready to pounce, bristles raised in defense.

The screaming of the girls suddenly reached an all-time high as the snake slithered towards freedom, obviously wanting to escape the chaos that it had been faced with. Sara turned into a blubbering mess, squealing uncontrollably at the sight of the scary looking creature in front of her.

"Sara, stop screaming!" Jack exclaimed. "The snake will freak out and strike at you!"

Those were the words that she needed to hear and they actually managed to stop all the girls from carrying on in such an over the top frightened manner.

"Our cat often brings snakes into the house!" Jackie

explained, trying to calm everyone down. "The other week he even dropped one on the lounge chair right next to my brother!"

Sara cried. "How on earth can you live in a place like this?"

"You've got to be kidding?" Alex replied in an amazed tone. "This is the best place ever! I'd love to live here!"

The expression on Sara's face quickly changed from horror to humiliation. Rather than giving her sympathy and attention, she was being made to seem pretty silly for reacting so foolishly. And then when she saw Blake high-five me and congratulate my quick thinking, her face glowed redder than ever.

"Oh, whatever!" she replied. "So, I'm scared of snakes. Isn't that pretty normal?"

Once again, Millie rolled her eyes towards me and then thankfully, Jackie broke the tension by inviting everyone into the dining room for something to eat. Her mom had prepared an amazing array of food, which was waiting for us on the table and as we were all starving, we eagerly sat down to enjoy the feast.

"That was really cool!" Blake exclaimed once more, glancing admiringly in my direction. "The only place I've ever seen a snake before is behind a thick pane of glass at the zoo. I never thought I'd see one up that close and especially on a living room floor. Do you think it was poisonous?"

We all looked towards Jackie, who we assumed would know something about it. "I think it was a red-bellied black snake," Jackie replied. "And yeah, they're really venomous. Our cat has definitely used up several of his nine lives since he was born, he's so lucky he hasn't ever been bitten."

"That was so awesome!" Alex commented again. And we all sat there munching away hungrily as we chatted about the excitement we had just witnessed.

Sara remained pretty quiet until we had finished eating and then someone suggested that Jackie should open her presents.

It was at that moment that Sara had a sharp change of mood. "Yes, I can't wait to see what Jackie's been given!"

She looked smugly around the group as we all left the dining table and headed out to the veranda, where the pile of wrapped presents waited to be opened.

"Save mine till last," Sara stated firmly, as she nudged it out of Jackie's reach.

As we sat watching, Jackie opened her gifts and we looked on with admiration at the lovely things she had been given. There was a gorgeous bracelet, a really cool hand bag, some cute pj's for the summer months, an iTunes gift card and some gift vouchers. The boys had chosen to give her some cash so that she could choose something for herself.

Millie and I were really pleased to see how much she loved our gift and also that the jacket fitted her so perfectly. She was especially pleased with the J pendant necklace that we had bought for her and she smiled at us gratefully.

"I've always loved your necklace, Julia and now I have one of my own! Thank you so much girls!" and she gave us each a big hug.

"Ok, now for Sara's gift," she exclaimed, smiling towards Sara questioningly. "I wonder what could possibly be inside this huge box."

We sat with anticipation, each of us wondering exactly the same thing. As I glanced at Sara, I could see that her smile really couldn't have become any wider as she waited expectantly for Jackie to open her present.

"Wow!!!" Jackie sighed in absolute astonishment as she removed the lid. Inside were several individually wrapped presents sitting decoratively amongst some pretty lilac tissue paper that had been scrunched up. As Jackie opened each parcel, the oohs and aahs from all of us looking on, continued with the unwrapping of each little gift.

There was a set of lip gloss, each one a different flavor, a box of expensive chocolates, a double pass to the cinema in town, a really pretty halter top and pair of shorts in contrasting colors and a gorgeous necklace that certainly was prettier than the simple J pendant that Millie and I had given her.

Just then, Jackie's parents arrived and the look of amazement on her mom's face echoed our thoughts completely. "Oh, my gosh, Jackie! You are such a lucky young lady! You've been given so many beautiful gifts. And are those the things that came out of that box?"

When Jackie nodded her head in acknowledgement, her mom continued, "Sara, you have really spoilt her. That was very naughty of you!" she exclaimed.

"Thank you so much, Sara!" Jackie hugged her tightly and then sat back looking at her gifts with huge delight.

"Oh, that's ok, Jackie!" Sara exclaimed modestly. "I'm glad that you like them!"

Shaking my head in wonder, I looked towards Millie whose eyes were still as wide as saucers at the sight of the extremely generous gift Sara had brought.

Then the silence that had enveloped all of us, was abruptly broken when Jackie's mom announced that it was time for birthday cake. Crowding together around Jackie for photos while her dad lit the candles, we all donned huge smiles as we called out, "Happy Birthday, Jackie!" We followed this by singing happy birthday to her and then sat down to the most delicious birthday cake I think I have ever tasted.

Soon after…as the sun was starting to set, it was time for the boys to leave. All the girls were staying for a slumber party. Jackie's parents had set up a tent in their back yard and had even gathered wood for a campfire. It was going to be the best night ever!

Jackie's Dad started the fire and we all sat around and sang songs. Then he brought out some marshmallows. We put them on sticks and toasted them in the fire. They were so delicious and it was really cool being able to sit there watching them gently sizzle over the flames.

We were all too full to eat much of the pizza they had ordered in, so we decided to play hide and seek in the dark. The laughter coming from everyone was mixed with squeals and yelps from some of the girls who were racing around on the grass. Then, all of a sudden, Millie said that she thought she could hear someone crying.

Glancing in the direction of the sobbing, I spotted Sara crouched into a ball and totally freaking out. We'd all forgotten about the snake, but she hadn't and she was actually shaking with genuine fear. I felt sorry for her, so I suggested we go back to the campfire where it was warm and not quite so dark.

"No, I want to go inside!" she cried in response.

We all looked at each other and sighed. It was clear that she was not going to be convinced to stay outdoors and when she reached the safety of Jackie's bedroom, she refused to come back out again. There was no alternative except for us all to traipse back down to the tent, bring our sleeping bags into the house along with Sara's and set them up on the lounge room floor.

"What are we going to do now?" asked Millie, her voice barely masking her disappointment.

"I know what we can do!" Sara replied with sudden enthusiasm. "How about some girly stuff? I brought my make-up kit so we can have heaps of fun with that! There's some really pretty blue eye shadow that would definitely suit the color of your eyes, Millie. Let's get it out and have a look. You girls can use whatever you want."

"Seriously, who brings their make-up kit to a slumber party?" This was the thought that was going through my head. But Sara's excited ramblings continued.

"Then we can borrow Jackie's hair dryer and straightener and straighten each other's hair!" she exclaimed with absolute delight. "I love straightening my hair, it looks so much better when I do!"

"Could this really be happening?" I shook my head in disbelief at the scene unfolding right in front of me.

"How did we go from camping with a campfire and running around in the dark, to putting on make-up and doing our hair? Don't get me wrong, I like to play around with make-up and make my hair look good, but we can do that anytime!"

I had to give her credit though! She was so good at manipulating situations to make herself happy and the center of attention. However, Jackie looked torn. It was obvious she didn't want to upset Sara but I could see by her false smile that she wasn't at all happy her slumber party had been hijacked.

To try and save the situation, I ran to get my iPod and put on some cool music. Then, within minutes, everyone was settled around Sara's make-up and had begun testing the different products that were stored in the large pink carry case.

The music certainly helped to lift everyone's spirits as well and before long, we were all singing to our favorite hit songs.

I was pleased to see that Jackie was laughing once again and having fun. There would be nothing worse than to have your party spoiled by one of your guests. But as it turned out, we all had a pretty good time.

The next morning, after very little sleep because Sara was too scared to close her eyes in case the snake came back, we dragged ourselves out of our sleeping bags so that we could head into the dining room for breakfast. Sara's mom had made pancakes and we sat around the table in our pajamas, talking and laughing about how much fun the party had been.

Unfortunately though, everyone's parents soon started to arrive and it was time to head home. Before leaving though, we all agreed to try and fit in as many dance practices as possible during the next few days at school. The final dress rehearsal was scheduled for later in the week and we still had lots of work to do before then.

As Millie and I hopped into the back of my dad's car, I overheard Sara commenting to some of the girls. "I can't wait for the musical! It's going to be amazing and I'm sure everyone will be in for a huge surprise!"

Just as I closed the door, I caught her glancing in our direction but the strange expression on her face carried a meaning that I couldn't quite fathom. She waved as we drove off but the cold look was what worried me the most.

Regardless of the party being hijacked by Sara, we had still thoroughly enjoyed it and now the musical was quickly approaching. I should have been full of excited anticipation but the sudden attack of nerves that I had been overcome with, caught me by surprise. Feeling tired and a little anxious, I leaned back against the head rest on the rear seat of the car and closed my eyes.

Oh no, NOT today....

The eve of the musical finally dawned and I had gone to bed early in order to get a good night's sleep. Our dress rehearsal had been a roaring success with every single item being performed almost to perfection. Miss Sheldon was beside herself with excitement. She seemed to think that it looked to be the best show the school had ever performed. At least since she had been teaching there, and she had huge expectations of a stand out extravaganza.

The tickets had all sold out and the office staff were asked to quickly print extras as well as hire more chairs to squash into the already very crowded auditorium. This was necessary to accommodate the overwhelming number of people who were keen to be a part of the audience. It appeared that almost half the town were coming and it was just lucky that the hall was big enough to seat everyone.

I rolled over in bed and closed my eyes, determined to fall asleep quickly so that the morning would arrive and I could begin the exciting day ahead. Then, what seemed like only a few minutes later, I was awakened by a noise outside my bedroom door.

Sitting up, I realized that it was our dog, Roxy scratching at the door and trying to get in. As I rubbed my eyes in an attempt to focus, I became aware of daylight streaming into the room from behind my curtain.

Glancing at the alarm clock that sat on the bedside table next to my bed, I rubbed my eyes once more. With a sick feeling in the pit of my stomach, I grabbed hold of the clock and looked at the time again.

"Noooo!" I screamed loudly. "This can't be happening!"

I slept in!

With my heart racing like the beat of a pounding drum, I frantically sprinted out of bed, opened the door and looked out into the hallway. Ignoring the eager tail wagging and expectant look from Roxy, I bounded towards the bathroom and turned the handle of the door. But it wouldn't budge.

"Oh no!" I grumbled loudly, then heard the familiar sound of my brother singing in the shower. "I need the shower!" I yelled desperately. "Hurry up!!!"

Of all mornings to have slept in! I just couldn't believe that my alarm hadn't gone off. I was sure that I had set it accurately the night before, thinking at the time I certainly didn't want to risk oversleeping and missing my bus.

"The bus! Oh, my gosh!" I yelled, running back into my bedroom to double check the time. The early bus was due in five minutes and there was no way I could get a lift to school. Because my parents both had a seven o'clock start on a Friday morning, I knew that they would have already left for work. I thought about my promise to Miss Sheldon, agreeing I would arrive early to help with all the setting up which still had to be done. It was blatantly obvious that I needed to get to school as soon as possible.

Deciding to go without a morning shower as I'd had one the night before, I threw on my clothes and grabbed the bag that

I had already packed ready with everything I would need to take. Bolting down the stairs, I literally flew out the front door.

I don't think I have ever sprinted as fast as I did that morning. But to my huge dismay, I arrived at the bus stop out of breath, only to see the bus pulling away from the curb. Yelling for the driver to stop, was a waste of time and I anxiously watched the bus head down the street.

Dropping my bag on the ground in disgust, I stood there in despair racking my brains for a solution. Waiting for the next bus was not an option; that would get me to school just before the bell and I needed to arrive much earlier than that, in order to get all the necessary jobs done.

It was then I decided that I would have to walk. A fast walk along with running some of the way, would be the quickest alternative. And besides that, I was too worked up to stand there waiting 40 minutes for the next bus to arrive.

So off I took and just when I realized that I was actually making pretty good time, I felt some droplets of water on my face. Looking up, I spotted an accumulation of very dark clouds heading my way so even though I was already breathless, I forced myself to run.

However, I was unable to beat the rain. At first it was a light sprinkle and then gradually became slightly heavier. Within minutes though, it was bucketing down and I was absolutely drenched.

Running through the school gates and trying to avoid a huge puddle of water that sat right in the middle of the driveway, the rubber bottom of my shoe skidded wildly. Feeling as though I was skating on ice, I slid recklessly across the slippery surface, desperately trying to maintain my balance. But then with an uncontrollable yelp, my legs went out from under me.

I hit the hard asphalt with a thud, landing flat on my back, my head coming down heavily with a bang. Dazed and very sore, I managed to stand, the rain still pouring down around me. By this time, I was absolutely saturated and had mud all over me along with a scraped and bleeding knee. I could already feel the throbbing lump starting to form on my head and I hobbled cautiously towards the Performing Arts building, not wanting to slip over again.

When I entered, the room was full of excitement and noise. People were scattered all over the place in various stages of preparation. I ducked under a ladder that was blocking the entrance and looked up to see Blake helping to hang a large banner.

"Not a good idea to walk under ladders, Julia," Miss Sheldon warned when she noticed me trying to weave my way inside the door. "That brings bad luck you know!"

"As if I haven't already had enough bad luck today!" I muttered miserably to myself.

Then all of a sudden she did an abrupt double take. "Julia!" she exclaimed in a worried tone. "You're soaking wet! And what have you done to yourself?" She looked down at the blood oozing from the graze on my leg which now appeared much nastier than I had originally thought.

I could feel tears starting to form in the corners of my eyes but then noticed Blake climbing down the ladder towards me so I quickly brushed them away.

"I'm alright," I said trying to muster a convincing tone. "I missed the bus, so I decided to walk to school. But it started to pour with rain and then I slipped on a puddle in the school driveway."

"I'll get a first aid kit," Miss Sheldon quickly replied. "I don't really like the look of that gash on the side of your knee. I hope it doesn't need stitches!"

"Oh, I'm sure it'll be fine," I said bravely, as I took a sip of water from the bottle that Blake had handed me.

"Blake, see if you can get something to press onto that gash and stop the bleeding. I'll be back in a minute." Miss

Sheldon raced towards her office, on the way picking up a roll of paper toweling that had been left on a chair. "Here you go, use this," and she threw it towards him.

I sat down while Blake held strips of the toweling firmly on my leg as I miserably watched pools of water dripping onto the floor around me. In no time though, Miss Sheldon was back and had cleaned the wound with antiseptic and wrapped my leg in a sterile bandage.

"It looks like you fell on something sharp," she commented. "We'll have to keep an eye on that. But in the meantime, why don't you try and dry off. There's some towels in the cupboard in my office and there might be some clothes in there that you can change into."

"Thank you, Miss Sheldon!" I replied gratefully. "I actually have a change of clothes with me. And at least my back pack

is waterproof, otherwise everything would be completely soaked, including my costume for tonight."

Millie then spotted me and raced over, a worried expression on her face. Rubbing my head tenderly, and wincing with pain, I explained what had happened.

When she realized that along with everything else, I also had a huge lump on my head, she ran to get some ice from the kitchen and then grabbed a couple of towels from the cupboard in Miss Sheldon's office.

After putting on dry clothes, I gratefully accepted a cup of hot chocolate and a breakfast bagel that had been provided for everyone who had offered to help that morning.

Holding the ice pack to my head, I looked down at the tight bandaging on my leg and hoped that it wouldn't restrict my dance moves. "Maybe I can just take the bandage off later," I said to Millie. "The bleeding will have stopped by then and at least I'll have more freedom of movement!"

She looked at me with sympathy and commented in her usual positive manner, "Well, thank goodness you got here, Julia! The show just couldn't go on without you!"

Grateful for her caring friendship, I smiled warmly and sipped the soothing drink which was helping to make me feel much better. Then with a determined resolve, I got to my feet and set myself to work. There was lots to be done and I knew that I needed to get started. We had a show to perform and nothing was going to stop it from being the best show ever. We had all worked so hard and I knew that it had to be a roaring success!

I spent the morning helping as much as I could. Although the throbbing pain I was feeling in my head had seemed to intensify, I focused my thoughts on the celebrations we would be having later that night, over the wonderful show we had performed.

And then suddenly out of the corner of my eye, I saw Sara Hamilton walk into the room.

Overwhelmed...

"Oh, Julia!" Sara wailed, as she headed in my direction. "I just heard about your accident. Will you be able to dance tonight?"

"Yes, I'll be fine," I abruptly assured her.

"Are you sure?" she asked, exhibiting what looked like a semblance of sympathy. "I wondered if you might be out of action! That would be such a terrible shame after all your hard work."

"Nothing will keep me off that stage tonight, Sara!" I declared in a determined voice.

"I thought it would have to be something terrible for you not to perform," Sara responded. "After all, you're pretty much the star of the show, of the dancing segments, anyway."

"Sara you have the lead role in our dance now, but regardless, it's a team effort and I think everyone will be stars tonight," I stated firmly.

I really wasn't in the mood for her games and hidden meanings. I just wanted to focus on getting organized and right then, I had a splitting headache and a really stiff and sore knee.

"By the way," Sara added. "Miss Fitz wants to see you. It's about the headbands for the girls' hair that you were meant to bring with you today."

"The headbands?" I asked, a sinking feeling forming in the pit of my stomach.

"Yeah," Sara replied. "Remember I gave you the message

from Miss Fitz yesterday afternoon? She arranged for your neighbor to do some last minute sewing and you were meant to bring them with you to school today."

"Sara, I don't remember you telling me that," I said, looking at her in complete puzzlement.

"You'd better go and see Miss Fitz," she replied. "She's freaking out in there because a lot of people haven't followed through with various commitments that they're responsible for. Miss Fitz and Miss Sheldon are complaining that some of the committee members should have been more organized."

Approaching her office apprehensively, I could see as I entered that Miss Fitz appeared quite stressed. "Miss Fitz," I stammered hesitatingly. "Sara said that you wanted to see me."

"Julia, please tell me that you brought those head pieces to school with you today?" We need them to keep the girls' hair pinned back. That dance that you choreographed for them has their hair flopping around everywhere and this is the last finishing touch."

"I know they need them, Miss Fitz but I wasn't aware that I was responsible for collecting them."

Just as she was about to take a deep breath and probably let fly with an angry retort, I asked if I could use the phone to call my mom. "She should be able to call in and pick them up," I explained hopefully.

"OK, and please be quick, there's still lots to do!"

Sighing with relief, I put the phone down a few minutes later. Mom had agreed to get the head pieces. I just prayed that our neighbor was at home. I knew that she usually headed off to visit her sister on Friday afternoons and often stayed there for dinner. But hopefully she might have left them out for someone to collect.

I crossed my fingers and sneaked out of the office, deciding that I should stay out of the way of my drama teacher. But I understood how stressful the whole situation was. Organizing something that was the magnitude of our school musical was a mammoth task and any number of things could go wrong.

Thinking again of Sara's words, I tried to recall her mentioning the message the day before but had no memory of it whatsoever. "Am I really becoming that forgetful?" I wondered. "Or is there just too much on my mind right now?"

As I thought about it some more, desperately searching through my memory banks, I could not bring myself to recollect Sara giving me the message from Miss Fitz.

Looking in Sara's direction, I could see her in a corner of the hall, laughing with Blake and some of the other boys. They were obviously enjoying her company and she was definitely thriving on the attention they were giving her.

She must have felt my eyes on her because she abruptly glanced my way and then with a little smirk, turned her back on me to refocus on the group of boys once more.

A feeling of doubt started to weave its way through my mind and tingles of apprehension began to build. Trying to force the worried thoughts away, I headed towards Millie and a group of other girls who were busy with the list of jobs that still had to be done.

Still absorbed in my thoughts, I failed to notice a wooden box that had been left lying in the middle of the floor. It was only small and the tawny brown color blended in with the floorboards beneath it. I didn't realize it was there until it was too late and I felt myself suddenly being propelled into mid-air. Desperately trying to regain my balance, I let out a loud yelp. This is something I have a bad habit of doing and rather than avoiding attention, it always alerts everyone around me. Of course, this occasion, was no different from any other and my squeal of fright drew all eyes towards me.

Landing heavily on top of the box, I could not stop the tears that began to flow down my cheeks. The humiliation and embarrassment of everyone staring at me and rushing to see if I was ok, was just too much to bear; that and the sharp pain that was added to my already throbbing leg. But the worst part of all was Sara's voice over all the others, "Oh my gosh, Julia! What is wrong with you today? I hope you don't fall over in our dance tonight! Are you sure you're going to be alright to perform?"

Throwing a black look in her direction, I didn't trust myself to reply for fear of bursting into a crying fit and embarrassing myself even more.

As Millie helped me to my feet and then to a nearby chair, the feeling of overwhelm that had engulfed me was like a bottomless pit I was frantically trying to climb out of.

The day I had been looking forward to for so long, had gone from bad to worse and I desperately hoped that no more terrible things would happen!

A Math Comp, of all things...

"You'll be fine, Julia," Millie said in her usual cheery voice. "Everything will go perfectly well tonight, you just wait and see!" I looked gratefully at my friend, very much wanting her to be right.

I had no time to focus on it any further though as there was still so much to do and to add to that, some of us had to be back in class straight after the morning tea break. A group of kids from our grade had been selected to enter a state-wide Math competition which just happened to be scheduled for the same day as the musical. This had been an oversight by our teacher who hadn't realized that the musical was also on that day. But because she had arranged for the school to pay the administration fee for each of the entrants, we were expected to be there. She gave us the condition that if we wanted to have the day off class to help out with the musical, then we had to do the Math comp.

"It's not fair," complained Millie as we hurried to the classroom where the competition was to be held. "This wasn't our choice! Why couldn't it just be left to all the math nerds in our grade? Why did they have to include us as well?"

"I think they were short of kids to enter," I replied. "But Math is my worst subject. I can't figure out why they chose me."

"Even though it's your worst subject, you're still good at it!" Millie exclaimed. "Better than me, anyway!"

"I thought this day couldn't get any worse!" That was the last thought in my mind before I sat down to focus on the paper in front of me. Rolling my eyes and sighing with impatience, I decided just to do the work and get it finished as soon as possible. We had planned one last rehearsal with our dance troupe and I was keen to get back to the buzzing excitement in the hall. Attempting to ignore my throbbing leg as well as the pain coming from the lump on my head, I looked down towards the Math questions on my desk and tried to concentrate.

Not feeling at all well...

Can things get any worse?...

Rushing back to the hall afterwards, Millie and I complained about the hard Math questions that had been included, especially towards the very end. The last few were so complicated.

"I skipped several of them," I admitted. "They were way too hard! And I'm certainly not looking forward to getting my result, that's for sure! If we're ever asked to do one of those competitions again, I'm just going to refuse!"

Millie agreed with me but on entering the hall, we quickly put the Math comp behind us. The seating and decorations were finally all in place and Miss Sheldon was directing a group of kids on the stage who were having a last minute rehearsal.

I scanned the hall, looking for all the members of our dance troupe so that we could also have a final rehearsal. We'd been discussing it that morning and had planned to meet up just after the lunch break, but they were nowhere to be seen.

"Maybe they're all out the back or in the dressing rooms. I'll race out and have a look." I watched Millie head off to look for them and just as I was about to search the adjoining rehearsal room, Miss Sheldon called me over. "Julia!" she said, "Just the person I was looking for!"

"Yes, Miss?" I replied questioningly.

"I'd like you to come with me. The junior girls need a last minute practice and I also need you to help me with the Grade Five item. There's still kids who could do with some extra help and I think one more run through is really going to benefit them."

The look of dismay on my face must have been obvious. "Aren't you feeling well?" she queried. "Is your leg a problem? Perhaps you should be at home resting it!"

"Oh no," I replied quickly. "My leg is fine." There was no way I was going to tell her that it was actually quite painful.

If I did, I was worried that she'd ban me from performing.

"I was just going to have a last rehearsal with the kids in my dance group," I tried to explain, but her stressed expression prevented me from continuing. "It's ok, though! I know the dance really well, they can just go ahead without me."

Trying to sound convincing, I followed her into the rehearsal room where the group of junior girls were waiting. I thought anxiously of Millie and the others, knowing they would be wondering where I was but I didn't dare leave to go and tell them. Miss Sheldon was a great teacher, but when she was stressed or angry, we all knew we just had to be quiet and do as we were told.

Thankfully, it didn't take long to get the junior girls in order and by the second run through, they had pretty much perfected the mistakes they'd been making. With a huge sigh I then moved onto the Grade Five kids, many of whom were racing crazily around the hall by that stage.

There were some pretty hyperactive boys in that group and they could not sit still, let alone follow instructions and it took all my strength not to start yelling at them to be quiet and listen. I was relieved when Miss Sheldon came over and told them off. That finally managed to calm them down and we were able to run through their entire item.

Just as we finished and I was about to go and look for Millie and the others, I heard an unmistakable voice. "Julia, where have you been?" We've been working our butts off trying to get our dance perfect and you didn't even bother to show up! Do you want our dance to be a success or not?"

The uncomfortable looks on the faces of all the others, just added to my humiliation. "I had to help Miss Sheldon," I tried to explain.

"Yeah, right!" I could feel my face turning bright red at Sara's abrupt remarks. "You're such a teacher's pet! You'll do anything to get on side with the teachers, even if it means letting your team down. Unbelievable!" And with a flick of her long blonde hair, she strode off towards the change rooms.

I looked towards Millie who just rolled her eyes and said, "Don't worry about her, Julia. You know the dance so well, we'll be great tonight, let's just go and get ready."

Feeling upset for what seemed like the umpteenth time that day, I slowly walked towards the change room door. I knew that the junior school kids were opening the show and I needed to be back stage to help them into their costumes. Taking a deep breath, I tried to muster some enthusiasm as I entered the bustling room that was filled with girls at different stages of preparation.

I suddenly looked at my watch. Seeing a few girls in the midst of getting their hair and make-up done, reminded me of the missing head bands and I anxiously hoped that my mother would make it in time.

The girls were expecting to wear the head pieces and apart from the decorative effect they created, they really were needed to help keep their hair tied back. With the throbbing in my head becoming worse, I walked over to the dressing area to assist the remaining girls with their costumes and make-up.

When they were finally organized, I decided I had better get dressed myself. If I didn't hurry, I would never be ready on time.

Searching frantically for my back pack, I scoured the area where I thought I had left it when I had arrived that morning. My memory of the morning's events was pretty foggy and I couldn't remember exactly where I had placed my bag. The change room was in chaos at that point. There were girls, teachers and helpers everywhere. Everyone was at different stages of getting ready and Mrs. Jackson was trying to keep the noise to a minimum.

"Sssshhhh, girls!" she was saying in a firm voice. "Please keep your voices down. It is way too noisy in here!"

By that stage, the room was totally frantic with excitement, the big night had finally arrived and girls in tutus, leotards and a variety of different costumes were lining up to get their make-up and hair done. I thought fleetingly about the head pieces for the younger girls and looked with concern at the clock on the wall, hoping that my mom would soon arrive.

"Millie," I called, when I spotted her and the other girls from our dance group assisting each other with applying mascara and lipstick.

"Can you please help me find my bag? I'm sure I left it in here this morning after getting changed, but I can't see it anywhere."

"Julia! I was wondering where you were and look at you! You're not even dressed yet. You need to hurry!" Millie's worried look made me feel even more anxious.

There were bags and costumes and props scattered all over the place, it was no wonder I couldn't see my bag but after a few minutes of searching, Millie finally handed it to me, "Here it is! I found it hidden under a pile of gear in that corner over there."

Frowning, I answered, "I could have sworn I left it over by the door."

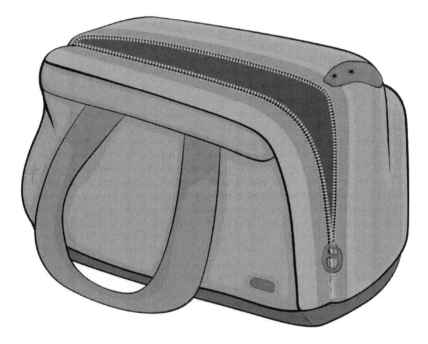

Millie shook her head and said, "Everything is such a mess in here. I'm surprised I found it at all!"

Casting my confusion aside, I quickly rifled through my bag, looking for the hip hop outfit that I had carefully folded and placed in there the night before, along with my shoes and accessories. But to my horror, it quickly became obvious that the outfit was missing.

Pulling everything out, I threw each item singly onto the floor, desperately hoping that the clothes I needed were hidden amongst my other bits and pieces. At the bottom of my bag, were my shoes and the long socks that we had all planned to wear, but there was no sign of the outfit I was looking for.

"NO!!!" I cried out.

"What's wrong, Julia?" Jackie had heard my distressed call and came over to see what the problem was.

"My clothes aren't in here! But I'm sure I packed them last night!" I flopped down on the floor, tears springing from my eyes. The day I had looked forward to for so long had gone from bad to worse. And I wondered how everything could have gone so terribly wrong.

"Fifteen minutes till show time, girls!" Mrs. Jackson was calling out. "I will need to start getting you lined up in your groups, so quickly finish getting ready.

I looked towards Millie and Jackie in despair. "What am I going to do?" I wailed.

"Julia Jones, aren't you even dressed yet?" Mrs. Jackson was looking at me with an expression of incredulity on her face. "Hurry up! There's no time to waste!" Shaking her head, she turned her attention to some younger girls who were trying to pin their hair back.

"Aren't these girls supposed to be wearing head pieces?" she asked no one in particular.

I didn't respond to that, thinking that I had much more important things to worry about than the girls' hair. How on earth was I going to be able to go on stage without my costume?

"What's wrong, Julia?" Sara's voice rang in my ears. "You're still not dressed! Have you decided not to perform?"

I was sure that her tone was full of sarcasm but as I turned to face her, I couldn't help but notice how pretty she looked.

Her glowing blonde hair was slicked back into a high pony tail and the bright red lipstick adorning her lips, set off her olive complexion beautifully. She looked so good in the outfit that had been designed for us all, and I felt overwhelmed with disappointment at the thought of not being able to take part.

"Julia, you can wear this!" the unexpected sight of the familiar shimmering blue fabric in Millie's hands was the answer to my prayers.

"Oh, Millie! Where did you find it?" I asked, barely daring to breathe.

"This one belongs to Annie Thompson. When she broke her leg, she returned it to Miss Sheldon and I spotted it in the cupboard in her office when I went looking for towels this morning."

"Oh, my gosh, Millie!" I said gratefully. "You're a life saver!"

I glanced in Sara's direction and noticed the surprised look on her face. "Looks like I'll be going on after all, Sara." I said in a curt tone and quickly rushed to get changed.

I tried not to think about the throbbing pain still emanating from my head as well as the gash on my knee. I had pulled the blood soaked bandage off and although my leg really needed to be covered up, I couldn't very well go on stage with a horrible looking bandage wrapped around it.

By the time I was dressed, there was no time to worry about make-up. I swiftly tied my hair back into a pony tail and regardless of the fact that it wasn't as neat as I would normally like, it just simply had to do.

Disaster...

After directing the younger girls onto the stage for their opening dance, I took a deep breath and watched from the wings, praying that even without their head pieces, they would exhibit the same killer performance that they had in the rehearsal.

The deafening applause at the end of their dance was music to my ears and I congratulated them all as they skipped off the stage.

The next act was performed by Liam, and his incredible voice poured out into the auditorium.

The other singers were almost as good and I marveled once again at the talented kids in our school.

The following performances were met with just as much enthusiasm from the audience. Then peering out into the crowd, I spotted my parents and my brother, Matt sitting near the front row. I assumed that my mom hadn't been able to get the head pieces, but as it turned out, the girls managed to get through their dance regardless, so I was very grateful for that. Although I still felt bad over their obvious disappointment at not being able to wear the sparkling addition to their costumes.

Finally, it was our turn and my stomach churned with anxiety and nerves. As we raced out onto the stage to form our positions before the curtain went up, Sara turned to me and said, "Break a leg, Julia!"

"What?" I frowned.

"That's for good luck," she smirked and then faced the audience whose applause was deafening once again.

We lunged into our routine, with Sara in the front row, doing the somersaults that she was so good at and as usual, her precision and timing were excellent. The applause erupted again and with a flick of her long pony tail, she executed a very tricky interchange with Alex and then moved to the back.

Alex attacked his moves with his usual gusto and the sharp, expressive movements which made him the stand out hip hop dancer that he was. I felt a rush of pride at being a part of such a cool routine but just as I moved to the front position, I felt my leg give way under me.

It was a completely involuntary reaction and one I was powerless to prevent. I was supposed to kneel down and support the weight of one of the smaller girls on my bent knee but unfortunately it was the leg that I had injured that morning.

There was no way I could bear her weight and the sharp pain caused my knee to drop just as Abbie pressed down on it to raise herself into the air. With a gasp from the audience, she went tumbling to the ground. Bright red with embarrassment, she glared at me in horror and all I could do was help her up and try to resume the timing and movements of the routine going on around us.

Fortunately, Abbie had no trouble getting back into rhythm, but I just seemed to lose my place and was not able to recover. As if in slow motion, I felt myself limping around the stage after the others and then looking down, I realized that blood was oozing from my leg and onto the floor.

I tried to ignore it and focus on the moves that I knew so well, but I was simply unable to get it together. Gratefully, Millie took over my spot and I moved once again to the back row, trying to camouflage myself amongst the others.

The scene around me was almost surreal and I felt as though I were a spectator watching the event unfold from afar. The swirling, twisting and turning of the dancers in front of me, along with the steady thumping beat of the latest hip hop song that everyone knew so well, all seemed to mesh together into a whirlpool of crazy colors and sounds.

Then, feeling a slight nudge in my lower back, I was pushed towards the front of the stage. An instant flash of recall had me leaping into the air.

Everyone still considered this moment the highlight of our routine. It was the grand finale and my chance to relinquish my status as actually being a decent dancer and choreographer.

Flinging my arms and legs forward, I came down onto the stage, one foot at a time. Then reminiscent of that morning's episode in the school driveway, rather than gripping onto the stage in a final dramatic stomp, my foot slid forward and just kept on going until my whole body landed horizontally on the floor with a loud bang.

In a blur of dizziness, I sat up and looked around then saw that I had slipped on a pool of blood; blood that had oozed from the gash in my knee and onto the stage. At that very moment, I was overcome with a sudden rush of nausea and unable to stop the sudden convulsion, I vomited all over the floor in front of me.

Too terrified to open my eyes, I wished I could turn back the clock. Back to the day of our dress rehearsal when everything had gone so smoothly. My final leap had been the high point of the day, where even Miss Sheldon and also Alex our expert hip hop dancer, had congratulated me on my performance.

I dared to glance fearfully out into the audience. Everyone appeared aghast and I could see the shocked expressions of my mom and dad. Then, realizing I was surrounded by worried faces peering down at me, everything suddenly went black.

What is Sara really up to?...

The next thing I remember was my mom's voice. "Julia, Julia!" Are you alright, darling? Julia…"

I had gazed at her briefly before blacking out once more and then awoke in a strange bed, my mom, dad and brother by my side.

After collapsing so dramatically on stage, I'd been rushed to hospital in an ambulance where I'd had to spend the night for observation.

When I opened my eyes, my mom hugged me tightly, the relief obvious in her eyes. "I'm so glad that you're ok, sweetheart!"

"You had us really worried, Julia!" my dad continued with concern.

And then of course, a typical comment from my brother, Matt. "What a finale, Julia. You were awesome!"

Mom looked at him crossly which quickly wiped the grin from his face. Trust him to try to joke around, even at the most inappropriate times. I certainly wasn't laughing but I sure was glad to have my mom and dad there with me.

When I was finally allowed to leave the hospital, I couldn't wait to get home to the safety of my room and I quickly climbed the stairs, declining any offers of help from my parents.

I could not believe that the night I had been looking forward to for so long had ended up so badly. All the time and effort I had put in to getting our dance perfect was for nothing. Well, that's how it seemed to me. I had practiced and rehearsed constantly, just as much or even more than anyone else. And it had all ended disastrously.

After arriving home from the hospital, I spent the next 2 days in bed. I felt so embarrassed and humiliated and didn't want to face any of my friends ever again.

"Perhaps I could go to another school?" That was the question I silently asked myself over and over while trying to be brave enough to make the suggestion to my parents in the hope that it might be possible.

I knew they wouldn't allow me to change schools but I just did not know how I could possibly face everyone again. I decided that I must be the laughing stock of the grade and I really dreaded the thought of ever going back.

I replayed the entire events of that terrible day in my mind, right from the moment when I had woken up late and realized I had overslept. Thinking back now, I've come to the conclusion that it was doomed from the start. So many things went wrong and it just didn't seem fair.

As I lay there, I envisioned the smirk on Sara's face that I had seen so often. I felt totally convinced that she was not the girl I had originally thought she would be. Too many things had happened over the past weeks and I tried to piece the puzzle together.

A couple of events stood out in my mind. For one, the message from Miss Fitz about the head bands for the junior girls. I am positive that Sara never gave me that message.

Another issue was my missing costume for our dance. I'm sure that I packed it and since coming home, I've searched every possible spot in my room but it's nowhere to be seen. I know that I had it in my bag, and if that is the case then where did it get to? And where is it now?

I wondered if that mystery would ever be solved. I thought briefly about confronting Sara and asking her directly if she knew anything about it but I was sure that would be useless. She'd never admit to anything, even if she was guilty.

Just as I was trying to concoct a really good excuse for having the entire week off school, I heard a gentle knock on my door. Then to my surprise, Millie's smiling face appeared.

"Julia!" She came rushing over to my bed to give me a huge hug. "Are you ok?" she asked, with genuine concern. "I've been so worried about you! I wanted to come sooner but your mom said that you needed some time to recover before having visitors."

Just having Millie there, was instantly reassuring and I could feel my spirits rise. Then when she pulled a block of my all-time favorite chocolate out of her back pack, I couldn't help but grin widely.

"My favorite!" I exclaimed. "Thank you so much!"

"I know," she replied, watching me rip the wrapping open. "I was hoping it might cheer you up."

"It's so good to see you, Millie!" I responded, hugging her once more. "But I'm so embarrassed about what happened. How am I ever going to go back to school again?"

"Everyone was worried about you, Julia!" she quickly replied. "After the ambulance came, you were all that everyone could talk about. They were all really concerned. They'll be so happy to see you back at school tomorrow."

I looked away from her trying to hide the tears that had sprung to my eyes. "I really don't want to go back to school, Millie. I'm so worried about seeing everyone. It's all so humiliating."

"Julia, don't be silly. Everyone will be so happy to see that you're alright. And the musical would never have happened without you. Miss Fitz and Miss Sheldon are so grateful for all your help. They even made an announcement at the end of the night and everyone stood up and cheered. They all know how hard you worked to put it all together."

At that moment, I felt especially grateful to have Millie as my friend and I glanced towards the wall where I had my favorite photos attached to a board. In particular, I loved the shot my mom had taken of us while we'd been taking our own selfie. Just the sight of that image instantly put a smile on my face.

Keen to convince me that everything was okay, Millie continued on.

"Anyway, Julia, it was lucky that our dance was the last

performance. Everyone got to perform and apart from you collapsing, the show was a huge success. But so much of it was thanks to you!"

After a moment's silence, she questioned anxiously, "You ARE coming back to school tomorrow, aren't you, Julia?"

With a nod of my head, I gave her another big hug. But I was still concerned about Sara. I wasn't sure whether to mention her to Millie or not. Millie would probably say I'm imagining things and being completely silly.

I decided to keep my thoughts to myself. I didn't want to spoil Millie's visit. I was so glad that she was there and I forced myself to look forward to returning to school the following day.

Back at school...

Everyone really did seem pretty concerned when I turned up at school. A heap of kids surrounded me, asking if I was ok. The teachers all came to check on me as well.

It was so nice to see that they genuinely cared, although I really didn't want to talk about it at all. I had decided to label that day, 'My Worst Day Ever,' and I definitely wanted to put it out of my mind forever.

Some of the kids were already talking about the next musical, but I certainly was not interested in getting involved in that conversation. I think that I've had more than my share of musicals for a long time.

I avoided making eye contact with Sara during class that morning. The desks had been rearranged the week before and I was very glad not to be sitting next to her any longer. That definitely helped me to get through the morning. I just focused on my school work and tried not to think about her.

During our lunch break though, I could see Sara surrounded by her adoring fan club. That's what Millie called them anyway.

Since the musical, apparently everyone had been raving about how great her dancing was and commenting that she was the star of our routine. But I guess that was what Sara had wanted to achieve and she'd managed to get her wish.

Chatting with Millie and the others, I was glad that I had a nice group of friends whose company I could enjoy without having to feel anxious or worried about what they might do or say. That's what I needed to focus on, I tried to remind myself.

But then, without warning, I felt someone's eyes on me and turned towards the group of kids who sat huddled together in a nearby corner, absorbed in each other's animated conversation. With a sudden shiver of apprehension, I realized that Sara was staring in my direction. And I knew without doubt that she must be staring at me.

Her blue eyes were so intense right then and the look she gave was full of attitude. Draping her arm around Blake's shoulder, she pulled him close and whispered something into his ear. Her eyes never leaving mine, I saw them both laugh at her obvious joke. Feeling very uneasy, I looked nervously away.

I had no idea what was going on in her head or what had caused the animosity that she was directing towards me and the uncomfortable sensation I was feeling, continued. With a tingling of unease, I turned my back on the group and tried to refocus on the friends sitting beside me who were consumed by their own friendly chatter.

I decided that I should put Sara out of my mind. Although I wanted the mystery solved and my questions answered, I figured I should just focus on my real friends, the ones who I always felt comfortable with. And besides, perhaps it was all in my imagination.

Perhaps Sara had passed on Miss Fitz's message and I had simply forgotten about it. And perhaps my dance costume was just mislaid amongst all the chaos in the dressing room on the night of the musical.

Perhaps? Or perhaps not? I really didn't know what to think!

Then a few minutes later, from directly behind, I heard the sound of a familiar voice. "Hey, Julia! Good to see you back at school!"

As I looked towards the voice, a group of laughing girls suddenly emerged, heading in the direction of their classroom and I couldn't see who the voice had come from. I was fairly convinced that it was Sara who had spoken, but I wasn't completely sure.

The tone had been friendly enough, but I didn't know if there was a hidden meaning behind the words. Was she really happy to see me back at school or not? And was it actually Sara whose voice I had heard?

"Did you see who that was?" I asked Millie.

"Who what was?" she replied.

"I thought I heard someone talking to me," I answered thoughtfully. "But maybe I was imagining things."

Jumping tensely at the sudden shrill ring of the bell which signalled the end of lunch break, I glanced around once more. "Yes, it must have been my imagination," I repeated, looking around one last time.

Then I stood to follow Millie and the others back to class. I tried to get involved in their giggling and joking around, but I could not dispel the confused but foreboding sensation I had been overcome with.

Was Sara trying to be friendly or wasn't she? Did she have a hidden agenda or did I just have an over-active imagination?

Confused thoughts raced through my mind as I headed back to class.

Then, unexpectedly, I felt a light tap on my shoulder. Whipping my head around nervously, I gasped in surprise.

"Julia! I'm so glad to see that you're ok! We were all freaking out the other night!"

Blake's sparkling eyes and friendly smile were enough to make my heart melt.

I felt the tension ease away as we strode along the pathway and up the stairs towards our classroom, all the while chatting comfortably as we walked.

"I'm so glad I came back to school," I thought happily to myself, all thoughts of Sara disappearing temporarily from my mind.

But then I entered the room. And it was at that moment, I could feel the hairs on my arms stand on end. I looked questioningly up at Blake, who was still at my side laughing easily.

I was unsure what had caused the sudden chill I was feeling and rubbed my arms for warmth, attempting to fend off the cool draught that had abruptly appeared from nowhere.

It was when I happened to glance towards the back of the class, that I saw a pair of penetrating blue eyes drilling into my own. The expression that had crept over Sara's features was dark and forceful, but the disturbing thing was that her death-like stare was aimed directly at me.

Completely unaware of the look I was receiving, Blake left my side and sat down in his seat in the front row.

Tentatively, I made my way to my own spot and sat down, grateful to escape the wrath of her evil glare.

The uncomfortable sensation lingered however, and I was forced to turn to face her once more. Still staring directly towards me, I was sure that she had begun to shake her head. It was the slightest movement, barely noticeable, but definitely betraying a hidden meaning.

As I turned back towards the front of the room, I felt my throat become dry, while at the same time, confused and anxious thoughts flooded my mind.

Swallowing hard, I took a deep breath and tried to ease the nervous energy I had been overcome with. But for some strange reason, it continued to linger and I remained in my seat, eyes faced forward, not daring to look behind me again.

When the final bell of the day clanged loudly, I instantly stood, eager to leave the classroom as quickly as possible. But as I walked to the bus stop, I could not shake the sinking feeling that had lodged itself in the pit of my stomach.

***

What lies ahead for Julia Jones?
Will Sara be her friend or does she have something else in
store for Julia?

Find out in Book 2
Julia Jones' Diary – My Secret Bully

**Read what others are saying about Julia Jones' Diary -
Book 2...**

*-Love the book Katrina Kahler it is awesome, best book ever. I have
never read a book in 3 days and that's saying something because I
don't typically read that fast ever.*

*-This book is realistic, it's almost like I can feel it. I recommend
this book to everyone. I picked five stars because it was really
AWESOME!! It's good advice if you are getting bullied. I really
recommend this book!*

*If you loved Book 1, and would like to read the entire series,
you can buy the collection as a combined set at a
DISCOUNTED PRICE...*

Julia Jones Diary

Books 1 – 5

Available on Amazon and all large online book retailers...

Thank you
for reading my
book. If you liked
it could you please
leave a review?
Katrina

Please Like our Facebook page

to keep updated on the release date for each new book in the series...

www.facebook.com/JuliaJonesDiary

and follow us on Instagram:

@juliajonesdiary

Announcing a New Series!

*Find out what lies ahead for Julia and all her friends in a
brand new series...*

Mind Reader – Book 1: My New Life

OUT NOW!!

*This book introduces Emmie, a girl who unexpectedly arrives in
Carindale and meets Millie. But Emmie has a secret, a secret that
must remain hidden at all costs.*
*What happens to Julia, Blake, Sara and all the others and how does
Emmie's sudden appearance impact Julia and her friends?*
*This fabulous new series continues the story of Julia Jones but has
a whole new twist, one that all Julia Jones' Diary fans are sure to
enjoy.*

You can also read

MIND READER: Part One – Books 1, 2 & 3

at a *DISCOUNTED PRICE!*

Available on Amazon and all large online book retailers...

Announcing a New Series!

Many of the following books can also be purchased as a collection that includes a number of books in the series. Rather than buying each book individually, you can read the entire collection at a DISCOUNTED PRICE!
Just search for the titles on Amazon or your favorite online book retailer to see what is available...

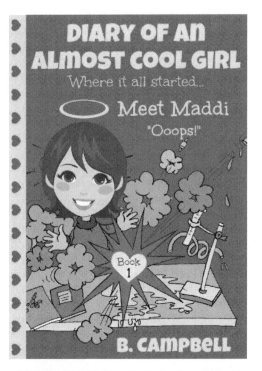

Diary of an
ALMOST COOL WITCH

Book 1

Bill & Kaz Campbell

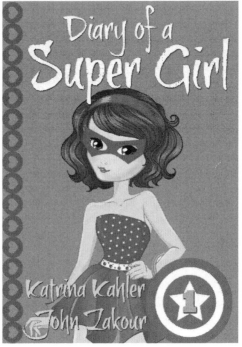

Diary of a
Super Girl

Katrina Kahler
John Zakour

1

Printed in Great Britain
by Amazon